Erotic Roma

First Time Gay - Hottie In The Pool

Sean Cockley

Jamie was just turning twenty with brown hair and brown eyes. He was five foot six with a tanned body. He had a smooth, hard chest. Muscles rippling through his flat stomach. Wearing a pair of white shorts that came down to his knees. Wearing black sunglasses he had a large net in his hand.

Jamie had worked for a man named Jimmy for the past few summers being a pool boy. Jamie's friends use to laugh at him until he told them how much money he made a week. Jimmy was an accountant and got paid extremely well there for Jamie got paid handsomely for the work he did around the house and making sure that the pool was clean every day. Jimmy didn't like to have one leaf, or even one small bug in his pool. Very picky about how clean the pool was.

"Jamie!" Jimmy hollered to him, coming through the back door to sit on the deck. The deck was big and at least fifteen feet off the ground. A set of stairs leading up from the pool to the deck so that whenever Jimmy had people over they liked how they could get out of the pool, walk up the stairs and have a few beers.

"Coming!" Jamie called back to him. Quickly getting out of the pool and setting the net down on the side he jogged up the deck stairs. When Jimmy called to him or to anyone he expected them to be there at his beckon call. Jamie didn't mind it because he was getting paid for it. Sometimes he would stay late and help out if there was a big party going on and he could see that Jimmy's friends didn't like it when he ordered them around. Jamie thought the only real reason they were friends with him was because of the amount of money he made.

"I want you to meet my younger brother Bradley." Jimmy told him, sitting down in a chair and letting the sun hit his white chest.

Jimmy had white/blondish hair. Light blue eyes and thin. Wearing a pair of blue jeans he loved the sun hitting his chest as he sat in his chair.

"This is Bradley. He will be staying with us for a week. Now I don't want you to do anything for him but if he messes up that pool you let me know how much harder you have to work and I will raise your pay until he's gone." Jimmy waved a hand in Bradley's direction.

Bradley was just as tall as Jamie. He was much younger then Jimmy was, which surprised Jamie a little. He looked to be in his early thirties where Jimmy was in his late fifties. He had black hair and dark blue eyes. When he smiled he had extremely white teeth, it made Jamie think that he bleached them every morning.

"Hi. I'm Jamie." He put his hand out and smiled at him.

"Bradley, of course." Bradley laughed, taking Jamie's hand and shook it. Holding on a few seconds longer then what was needed.

"He's adopted." Jimmy watched as they shook hands.

"Oh, so you aren't real brother's then." Jamie didn't mean to hurt anyone's feelings, knowing it sounded rude.

"We are in here." Jimmy put his hand over his heart and gave Jamie a smile. Letting him know that he hadn't been out of line.

"Great, what are you here for?" Jamie asked him thoughtfully, trying to get a conversation started.

"I come down once every few years. I figured this would be the year I would stop in and see how Jimmy is doing. Looking at the house and the many things he has I would have to say he is doing good for himself." Bradley looked around, he liked the view of the yard and the pool from where he was standing.

"I just never seen you before and I've been working a few years for Jimmy well summers." Jamie pointed out to him.

"Yeah, we never would have met before. I usually come visit in the winter time. Its always good to see him then just talking to him on the phone." Bradley told him, nodding his head.

Jamie wondered why Jimmy never talked about Bradley if they talked on the phone a lot. He would think that he would have overheard Jimmy talking about his brother at parties and functions but not once has he heard Jimmy talked about him.

"Have you cleaned the pool yet?" Jimmy asked him.

"That's what I was getting ready to do when you called me up here." Jamie explained to him quickly, seeing that was a sign to get back to work.

"Remember I don't want to see a single thing in that pool that's not suppose to be there." Jimmy warned him.

Jamie heard Bradley laugh lightly but he didn't say anything. It was none of his business why Jamie was really there. The only thing he cared about was getting to work and being done for the day. He had a date that evening and he didn't want to be late. It reminded him that he had to ask Jimmy if he could borrow the mustang for the night since he didn't have anything to drive himself.

Heading back up the stairs quickly he saw that Jimmy and Bradley weren't outside anymore. Sighing heavily he went back down to the pool and knew he would see Jimmy later on at that point he would ask him.

Jamie got back into the pool, loving the cool water rising up his legs and the deeper he went into the pool the higher the water went up.

Another good thing about the job he was glad that when it was hot outside he had a way to stay cool. Surprised that Jimmy would want his pool cleaned everyday all his friends and family would think it was sparkling clean, they didn't know Jimmy. If he saw a speck of dirt at the bottom of the pool or something almost microscopic he would freak out and probably fire him.

Usually cleaning the pool took him three hours to do and then he would be done. If he had nothing to do or someone was using the pool Jimmy made them get out of the pool every two hours to have Jamie clean the pool or make sure that everything was fine with it. He was a neat freak and Jamie knew that if they were friends Jamie would tell him to stop worrying over the damn pool.

"So how long have you been working for my

brother?" Bradley asked him, jumping Jamie out of his thoughts.

Looking over at him he saw that Bradley was wearing a black speed-o. His body just as white as Jimmy's as he started getting into the pool.

"Usually Jimmy doesn't like people in the pool when I'm cleaning it." Jamie told him as nicely as he could.

"He's not here and we don't have to tell him that I was in here. I will let you continue cleaning, I promise I won't be in the way." Bradley told him with a smile attached to his face.

"This will be my third summer working with Jimmy." Jamie answered him as he continued cleaning the pool, moving the net around and seeing that he couldn't get much more he knew that he had to use the hose to suck up the dirt at the bottom of the pool. There wasn't much and it could hardly be seen but if he didn't use the hose across the whole pool Jimmy would know. He remembered when he did a half fast job the first week he started working for Jimmy and he pointed at some spots that he had missed. He hollered at Jamie and told him that if he couldn't do the work then he would have to leave. Grumbling about how much money he was spending on a pool boy and he couldn't even do the job right.

"I know that my brother can be very demanding and picky at times." Bradley told him with a laugh.

Jamie didn't say anything to him. Not knowing him and not needing Bradley to be going back to Jimmy and tell him that he was talking about him. He would lose his job. He didn't really have too many problems when it came to Jimmy.

"Do you know what time he's going to be back home?" Jamie asked, changing the subject.

"Not until late tonight. I guess a client called him in a panic and he complained about what a late night it was going to be." Bradley shrugged his shoulders. Glad that he wasn't working for the week. He could kick back and relax.

"Damn." Jamie muttered to himself as he took the net out of the pool and pulled himself up out of the water.

"What's the matter? Maybe I can help out." Bradley offered.

"I have this date tonight and I have no car. I don't want to be taking the bus to a dinner and then a movie." Jamie blushed a little. He had his license he just had no car, thinking about getting one but not being able to afford anything real classy at the moment.

"If you want you can borrow my car." Bradley told him seeing that it was an easy fix.

"You don't even know me." Jamie laughed at him as he got the hose and hooked a wide tube up to it. A big box machine that filtered the dirt out of the water and put the clean water back into the pool.

"No but if Jimmy has kept you around this long then I figure you are good." Bradley laughed at him.

"That's true." Jamie shrugged his shoulders.

"You have lasted three summers so far and for my brother that's a big change. Usually his hired help lasts about a month because they can't stand him bossing them around all the time." Bradley chuckled.

"It doesn't bother me that he's bossy. He's not that hard to put up." Jamie laughed, saying something about Jimmy but the only thing that Bradley could go back to him with was that Jamie liked him as a boss.

"I have a red mustang. Its parked out front. When you need the keys just let me know." Bradley told him. Swimming the length of the pool the wide way instead of the long way so that he wouldn't be in Jamie's way.

"I have to wait for her to call me. I told her I would be working most of the day but would be ready tonight. Just waiting on her call." Jamie smiled at him, glad that he had the transportation for his date.

"The only thing I want to see is your license before you take off with my car. I don't need you getting pulled over and find out that my car is being held because you have no license." Bradley told him lightly.

"Sure, when I get done I will show you my license. Its in my dry shorts on the counter in the kitchen." Jamie stated. He had his license since Junior year in high school and always had a hard time getting his parents to let him borrow the car. Only one car and they both worked, not to mention they had their own activities going on when they weren't working.

"You live around here?" Bradley asked him.

"I live a few blocks away." Jamie told him.

"Don't tell me with your parents." Bradley laughed at him. Most young kids still lived with their parents and the way Jamie looked he still looked like a young kid.

"No, I live with a couple of friends." Jamie lied to him. He didn't want to have Bradley laughing at him. Just the way he had asked the question he knew that Bradley would laugh at him for living with his parents off the money that he was making from Jimmy. He wondered if Jimmy told him how much he was paying Bradley.

"That's good, these days you see young kids living at home and their parents still fitting their bills for the stuff they want and need." Bradley told him, hanging onto the side of the pool to take a break.

"Not all kids are like that. I have a kid brother who works two jobs and lives with our parents. He pays for his own things." Jamie lied to him. Though he did have a kid brother he only worked one job and the reason why he was still living at home was because he was going to college and couldn't afford his own apartment. He was kind of a geek and didn't want to live in the dorms.

"That's not too bad then. Good for him." Bradley nodded his head as he watched Jamie start in his direction.

Jamie tried to take his time working on the other side of the pool, letting Bradley work out for a little bit. He didn't want to be rude and tell Bradley he had to get out of the pool when he first went in.

Seeing that Jamie was headed his way he got out of the pool and stood there watching him clean the pool.

"Thanks." Jamie told him, glad that he moved without having to tell him to.

"Jimmy told me that I needed to stay out of your way so that you could do your job." Jimmy told him with a laugh.

"I would love to get my work done in a hurry. Though I do a thorough job. I don't want you thinking that I don't do the best I can." Jamie explained to him.

"I see that. My brother is very lucky to have someone like you. To be able to trust you while he goes to work and not have to look over your shoulder letting you know that you missed a few spots. That would drive me crazy." Bradley told him, he didn't like it when he knew what he was suppose to be doing and someone came over just to make sure he was doing it right.

"I look over the pool at least three or four times before I leave for the day." Jamie smiled, it drove him crazy the first few times of cleaning the pool but after getting yelled at by Jimmy he wanted to make sure that he made Jimmy happy the rest of the time. Quickly it got to be routine and he didn't even think about it.

"Do you ever stay here?" Bradley asked him raising one eye brow.

"What do you mean by stay here?" Jamie grinned at him. As he got out of the pool to turn the hose off.

"Like sleep over." Bradley asked him. Not sure if he was getting too personal with him. He was just trying to know more about him.

"Sometimes. I use the room off the side of the house when there are huge parties. Your brother has a lot of friend." Jamie laughed.

"I don't see them as friends. They are more like crooks, always borrowing money off of him and never paying him back but they come over here for the great food and drinks." Bradley lost the smile on his face.

"I thought that the reason they came over was because he was part a club. You know a rich club where as long as you were making the green and depending how much you were making you were on a list." Jamie was half joking but being serious at the same time.

"No, I mean the people that he sees as friends they have money. We all know they do but when they are broke or overdraw on their bank account then they turn to him. Jimmy's problem is that he's nice to the wrong people. He's nice to the people who screw him over." Bradley muttered.

"Maybe you should talk to him and let him know you're worried about him being used by his so called friends." Jamie advised him.

"Yeah right. Are you kidding me? Are we talking about the same Jimmy here? If I were to approach him then he would think I'm getting into his business and then all hell would break loose. If he was really worried about the money people owed him then he would speak up. He has no problem doing that." Bradley didn't tell him that he had tried the last time he was down. He spoke up in front of a crowd at Jimmy's last Christmas party and said that there were a bunch of leeches in the group. The last thing he remembered was waking up in the same room that Jamie used sometimes. It didn't help that he was half in the bag when he said something.

"Maybe he knows they really need the help." Jamie shrugged his shoulders, wrapping the hose up and putting it away. He pushed the machine up a small hill, thanking god that it had wheels and pushed it under the deck. Glad that there was plenty of space to store things so when it rained the equipment didn't rust in the rain.

"You done for the day?" Bradley asked him.

"Well I am going to take a dip now and look at the bottom of the pool to see if I missed anything." Jamie told him, getting back into the pool.

"You really go down there physically and see if you missed a speck of dirt?" Bradley laughed at him. Thinking it was really funny.

"If I don't and Jimmy sees something that I missed I'm going to get into trouble. That's the last thing I want. Jimmy has been good to me and I would like to keep my job." Jamie pointed a finger at him.

"It sounds strange to me but if that's part of your job and routine don't let me stop you." Bradley told him softly.

Bradley watched as Jamie went under the water, starting at one end of the pool. He was surprised that Jamie could see underwater. He couldn't swim underwater and look where he was going at the same time. He didn't like the water getting in his eyes as it was so he didn't swim underwater at all. He had always been that way since he was a kid.

Bradley continued watching Jamie until he was done. Estimating that it had been two hours until Jamie was happy with the way the pool looked.

"Wow, you do that everyday?" Bradley's eyes widened.

"Everyday." Jamie laughed at him. Seeing the shocked look on his face when he looked over at him. Getting out of the pool and sitting beside him.

"What do you like to do for fun?" Bradley asked, thinking he might stick around a little longer since he was beginning to like Jamie just by talking with him.

"I like to go play pool and darts. I like to watch movies and hang out with friends." Jamie thought about it for a minute.

As Jamie turned his head to look out over the yard he didn't notice that Bradley was watching him, looking over his body. Bradley had a small smile on his face and licked his lips as he continued to look over Jamie's body. He had made up his mind that he was going to spend another week. He knew that Jimmy wouldn't mind at all. They hardly got to see each other.

"I like to play cards, mostly poker. I bet money and usually win. My friends are real friends unlike Jimmy's we have a lot of fun together. They were sad when I came here to visit my brother. We hang out all the time though so they will get over it." Bradley shrugged his shoulders but he did wonder what they were doing from time to time.

"I have to go check my phone and change into dry clothes." Jamie told him, getting to his feet.

"Jimmy doesn't let you swim in the pool when you get done cleaning it?" Bradley asked him. Knowing that if he had done all that hard work he would take a few laps before getting out.

"I'm allowed to I just don't have the time right now. I'm waiting on a phone call and need to get some things done today." Jamie chuckled and shook his head as he climbed the deck stairs.

Going into the house he went to the kitchen. The floors were waxed and slippery on his bare feet. There was a long blue counter that ran around the kitchen. A small sink and a lot of cupboard space in the kitchen. The fridge was a double with a freezer underneath it.

Taking his dry shorts off the counter he reached into the back pocket and took his cell phone out. Hoping that there was a message from the girl he was going out on a date with. There was nothing yet. His heart started to sink. He hadn't had a date in a long time and he was hoping to have a good time.

Taking his wallet out of the other pocket of his dry jeans he opened it up taking out his license and going back out the door to the deck.

Bradley was sitting in the chair that Jimmy had been sitting in earlier that day letting the sun warm his chest. He hadn't even bothered putting on a pair of shorts. Sitting there in just his speed-o he saw the small bulge inside it. Blushing a little that he was looking at Bradley's cock.

"Did you need me for something?" Bradley asked him, feeling Jamie's eyes on him. Jamie blushed a little when he realized that Bradley had been looking at him while he was looking at Bradley's cock through the thin fabric.

"I just wanted to show you my license. You said something about needing to see it earlier." Jamie told him, handing it over to him.

Bradley took a close look at it and nodded his head, handing him back his license. He wanted to make sure it wasn't a fake.

"I never use to ask kids for a license. There

was a time when I just gave them the car keys and let them take the car for a few hours. The first time I got a call from the police telling me to come get my car and telling me how much I owed because the kid got pulled over for no license and I had to pay the bill to get my car back. That was the last time. I stopped trusting people with my car. It may sound funny and make me sound like I'm an uptight person but that's not the case at all." Bradley explained it to him.

"I wouldn't think that you were uptight. That's your car and you need to know you can trust people with your car. Something like that you never know if someone is going to take off with it." Jamie told him. Taking his license and holding it tightly in his hand.

"That girl call you back yet?" Bradley asked him.

"No, I have no calls at all." Jamie sighed heavily.

"Well if she cancels on you I'm going to be here by myself for at least a few more hours if you want to hang out." Bradley invited him to come back over.

"That would be great. Hey I gotta change and then head out. I'll come back later for the car." Jamie told him, heading back into the house.

"Hey Jamie." Bradley called to him.

"Yeah." Jamie asked, going back to the doorway.

"It was nice meeting you and thanks for putting up with me while you were cleaning. Jimmy thinks its bothering people if they talk and work." Bradley laughed.

"It wasn't a bother. I enjoyed the company for a change." Jamie smiled at him and disappeared back into the house.

Grabbing his dry shorts off the counter and putting his license back into his wallet he headed for the bathroom to change.

The bathroom was big. It had a shower, a bathtub and a hot tub all separate from one another. A washer and dryer stack able against the wall and a large sink that could have passed for a tub if Jimmy had any kids.

"Man I wish that I could afford something like this." Jamie whispered to himself taking off his shorts and putting on the dry ones. He was always amazed at the rooms in the house. Knowing Jimmy had money he sure didn't act it out in public. He had remembered going out to the pool supply store for some kind of chemical for the first summer. They looked for the cheapest Chemicals for the pool they found out quickly that it was an expensive store.

He laughed when Jimmy groaned about the price, complaining all the way to the cash register though he paid for it. Jamie laughed and laughed. With as much money as Jimmy had he would think that he would have no problem paying for the chemicals.

When he got out of the bathroom he left without saying goodbye to Bradley. Heading out the front door and starting the walk for his house.

Jamie waited until it turned seven o'clock that

night and saw that the girl wasn't going to call him. Sighing heavily he had nothing better to do but go back and hang out with Bradley. He knew that Bradley liked having someone to talk to. That was the only thing that he knew about Bradley really.

When Jamie made it to Jimmy's house he saw that Jimmy still wasn't home. Going around back because he never liked knocking on the door or ringing the doorbell he saw that Bradley was sitting by the pool looking at the water.

"She never called me." Jamie told him, laughing when he saw Bradley jump.

"I never heard you come up behind me." Bradley laughed with him when he realized it was Jamie.

He had a beer beside him. Taking the bottle and finishing it off he put it back down. Jamie saw that he was still in his speed-o surprised that he hadn't changed from earlier in the day.

"I was thinking about taking a dip. You want to join me?" Bradley asked him.

"I didn't bring any swimming shorts with me

tonight since I'm not on the clock." Jamie told him, seeing that would be a problem.

"You can always just swim around in your underwear. You have no idea how many times I have done that." Bradley chuckled.

Jamie shrugged his shoulders and took his jean shorts off. Standing in his black boxers he sat down and got into the pool slowly. Feeling the cold water surround his warm skin.

He shivered and felt his teeth shattering as he heard Bradley get into the pool beside him.

"You would think that Jimmy would want a heated pool. He has the money enough to get some heat in here." Bradley saw that Jamie was cold. He felt his own teeth chattering.

"Its not that bad when you start moving around." Jamie grinned at him and without hesitating he began swimming underwater and came up in the middle of the pool.

"You're crazy!" Bradley laughed at him.

"Just plug your nose and go under. It feels so much better when you resurface. You're not as cold that's for sure." Jamie told him with a smile on his face. Wiping his eyes.

The sun was setting as they were enjoying their time in the pool. They had stayed in the pool until it got dark.

When they got out of the pool Bradley started up the stairs to go inside the house. Jamie watched him.

"Are you coming or not? I can give you a pair of dry boxers. I am sure that we are almost the same size." Bradley offered him.

Jamie nodded his head. Neither one of them thought about grabbing a towel before the went into the pool. Jamie quickly walked up the stairs catching up with Bradley shivering.

They went into the house and Bradley turned on the kitchen light. Going to each room he turned the lights on. He never liked the dark and he noticed last night when he arrived that Jimmy still hadn't changed he liked living in the dark more then he did the light. Wondering how cheap his light bill was.

Bradley went and got a big towel and a pair of boxers out of the guest room that he was using. He threw the towel at Jamie and watched him dry off. He watched as he began patting down his boxers. Holding back a groan as he looked at Jamie's chest.

Jamie didn't see him looking at him as he dried his legs off and put the towel on the glass table in front of him.

"You want to toss that towel to me?" Bradley asked him.

"Oh sorry." Jamie nodded his head and took the towel in his hand. Tossing it over to him and he caught it with one hand.

"I don't like doing laundry if I don't have to." Bradley told him the reason why he had only got one towel.

"Me neither. I seem to be the only one who does the laundry." Jamie laughed, shaking his head.

"You do your friends laundry? Doesn't it feel weird? I would never do my friends laundry if they are capable of doing it you should make them do their own damn laundry." Bradley gave him a funny look.

For a minute Jamie forgot that he had lied to Bradley about where he lived. Almost getting caught in the lie.

"Well, I only do their laundry when the house is a complete mess and I see that no one had taken care of the laundry. Lately I just do the laundry that is in the basket in front of the washer. Its not that much of a bother." Jamie shrugged, not really thinking about it.

"The day I washed my friends clothes would be the day the devil said it was too cold in hell." Bradley shook his head back and forth.

"Well I am going to go change." Jamie told him, not knowing what else to say on the subject. Thinking about heading out before Jimmy got home. He didn't want Jimmy thinking it was weird that he was hanging around the house hanging out with Bradley.

Bradley watched him as he headed to the bathroom. Checking out his ass as he walked.

Watching it move from side to side he felt his cock begin to grow hard in his speed-o, not sure that he could have it go soft before Jamie came back out.

Going over to the sink and washing the few dishes that he had dirtied during the day and putting them in the dish strainer so that Jimmy wouldn't have to complain about having him stay for a week let alone when he found out that he wanted to stay longer. The last thing he needed was Jimmy to complain about having to pick up after him.

Jamie came out of the bathroom with a fresh pair of boxers forgetting his jean shorts out by the pool he moaned not wanting to have to go back down the stairs to grab his shorts.

"What's the matter with you?" Bradley asked, turning the water off to the sink.

"I forgot my shorts down by the pool and don't really feel like going to get them." Jamie knew he was being lazy and he wondered what Bradley was thinking.

Jamie walked around the counter and sat

down at the table. As Bradley turned to face him he couldn't help but look at the hard bulge inside Bradley's speed-o seeing that it was bigger then earlier when he got caught looking at Bradley's package.

"Do you like what you see?" Bradley asked him. Saying something this time. He had let it go the first time he caught Jamie looking at him, now he wanted to point out that he was noticing Jamie notice his cock.

"Um......I." Jamie thought about coming up with a lie but he wasn't good about lying when he was put on the spot.

"Its okay to tell me the truth." Bradley laughed at him, going over to him slowly and standing in front of him.

"If you want you can have a close up." Bradley teased him, starting to flirt with him.

"I'm not gay." Jamie blushed a little, wondering if Bradley was just playing with him. But Bradley hadn't moved away from him yet.

"How do you know you're not?" Bradley

whispered to him. Remembering that Jimmy had told him not to come onto the pool boy to let him do his job.

Jamie didn't say anything his eyes still on Bradley's speed-o. Seeing it was right in his face now he couldn't help but really look.

"Touch it." Bradley whispered to him again. Teasing him by moving closer to him.

"I don't know." Jamie told him, feeling his heart race and feeling his own cock start to get hard in the boxers that he let him borrow.

"Just try it." Bradley told him, clearing his throat.

When Jamie realized that he wasn't going to move until he at least tried touching it he reached his hand out slowly.

"It won't bite you, I promise." Bradley grinned at him. Seeing he was taking his sweet time reaching for his cock.

Jamie licked his lips because they were dry. When he put his hand against Bradley's cock and was surprised when he heard a moan escape his mouth.

"See you like the hardness." Bradley pointed out to him.

"I just didn't think you would be that hard." Jamie looked up into Bradley's face.

"You did that to me. I was checking out your ass when you went to go change into the boxers. I know that you were checking me out while I was sitting in the chair earlier getting some sun. You didn't see me noticing you looking but I sure noticed." Bradley explained to him.

"I never thought you to be gay." Jamie was surprised, he wondered if that was the reason why Jimmy never talked about Bradley to his friends.

"Not all of us are built perfect." Bradley laughed at him, seeing the look on his face.

"Sorry, I didn't mean it like that." Jamie told him quickly. He didn't want to offend Bradley in any way. He didn't need Bradley going to Jimmy and then getting fired for taking something that he said the wrong way.

"I know you didn't." Bradley stepped back

away from him.

Jamie got up from the chair and thought it would be best to go get his shorts. The thoughts that were running through his mind was going to make his own cock hard. A little nervous at the same time. He never had an actual gay encounter.

The second that Jamie got up from his seat is when Bradley put his hands on Jamie's waist. Jamie didn't look at him but he didn't pull away either.

"You will enjoy it. I can see it in your eyes that you are a little curious about what its like." Bradley told him softly. Bringing himself closer to Jamie and rubbing his cock against Jamie's. Feeling him get hard quickly.

"See how your cock likes mine?" Bradley asked him, pressing himself harder against Jamie. Grinding against his cock softly.

Bradley smiled when he heard Jamie moan, it felt good that his cock was getting some kind of attention. Thinking about the girl who stood him up.

"I've never done this before." Jamie told him, getting ready to pull away.

"I'll go easy with you. I promise I will go easy with you." Bradley told him quickly. He didn't want Jamie to leave now. It was almost like a tease. Knowing that Jamie's cock was hard too and the only way to make it soft was usually to jerk off.

Bradley grunted as he thought about Jamie jerking off by himself. Picturing it in the back of his mind.

"Please." Bradley was practically begging for Jamie to stay where he was.

Jamie didn't say anything for a moment. What seemed like five minutes had gone by with their cocks touching each other through thin fabric. Looking down at their hard cocks Jamie looked back up into Bradley's eyes. Saw him raise his eyebrows looking for an answer from him. Jamie couldn't find the words to say what he wanted so he nodded his head slowly keeping the eye contact with Bradley. He watched as Bradley smiled big.

"Alright then." Bradley told him as he

brought his mouth to Jamie's neck and began kissing it softly. Bringing one hand off Jamie's hip and putting it to the back of Jamie's neck holding onto it gently and pressing his mouth harder against Jamie's neck.

"That feels nice." Jamie whispered in his ear as they stood in the kitchen.

"Yeah? You like it?" Bradley asked him. When he took his mouth away from his neck and looked him in the eyes. He could see the lust and hornyness in his eyes. Knowing that he wanted anything, something to get himself off.

"Yes." Jamie groaned as he felt Bradley slide his hand into his boxers and began rubbing the head of his cock with his palm.

"I bet that feels good too." Bradley told him with a low chuckle.

"Oh god yes, that feels really good Bradley." Jamie told him. Glad that he had come back over. Wondering what was going to happen next.

"Good, that's what I love to hear. Come on pool boy we should take this into a different room in case my brother comes home. I am sure that he would be surprised to see the both of us making out and touching each other. Not sure how he would take it really." Bradley laughed, he would love to see the surprised look on Jimmy's eyes when he walked in through the door to see Jamie down on his knees sucking his cock in the middle of the kitchen floor.

Bradley took his hand out of Jamie's boxers.

"Please put your hand back in. I love how soft your hand feels against my cock." Jamie moaned, surprised at himself for the words that were coming out of his mouth.

"Look at you. A few seconds of a man touching your hard cock and you are already begging for more." Bradley laughed at him.

"Please." Jamie whispered to him, feeling himself blush. He had never asked anyone to take his cock in their hands. Never had to beg anyone.

"In the bedroom. The quicker we get to the bedroom the quicker I can touch your cock again." Bradley winked at him and walked away from him.

Jamie looked at the back door going out to the pool and looked at Bradley's back. If he was going to leave it had to be right then and there. Looking down at his cock he knew that it was throbbing inside his boxers. No one had ever made him feel the way he was feeling at that exact moment.

"Are you coming?" Bradley asked him. Looking at him over his shoulder.
Jamie didn't say anything, hurrying out of the kitchen and following Bradley to the room he was using while he was visiting.

"For a second there I thought you were going to leave me hanging. I saw you looking at the door thinking about bolting." Bradley told him before Jamie could even think of a lie.

"I just want to make sure this is what I want to try. Again, I have never done anything like this before. Not with a man. This is all very new to me. Never in my wildest dreams have I thought that a man could turn me on. My cock feels like its pulsing inside these boxers." Jamie explained to him.

"Its alright to be nervous. I was nervous my first time." Bradley admitted to him, glad that he had several lovers since then.

Jamie looked around the room and saw that there was a hot tub in the room. His eyes grew wide a hot tub in the bedroom. A big bed in the middle of the room and three flat screens hanging on the walls. Wondering why someone would need to have three of them.

"This is the room that I picked out. Jimmy bought all this stuff for me. When its football season I like being able to watch three different games going on at the same time instead of having to flip through the channels and go back and forth." Bradley saw the confused look on his face. Jamie nodded his head and thought it made sense.

Bradley walked over to the bed and sat on the edge of the bed. The satin sheets felt good on the back of his legs.

"Come here." Bradley told him, seeing that Jamie was stalling for a few seconds. He didn't know what was going through Janie's mind but he had hoped that Jamie wasn't having second thought.

Jamie looked at him and saw that Bradley wanted him to sit on his lap. Jamie walked slowly over to him and took a seat on one of Bradley's legs.

Bradley felt Jamie's arm go around his neck. Feeling his grip tighten on him like he might fall of his lap.

Bradley touched Jamie's cock through his boxers. Squeezing it gently and stroking it slowly. Hearing him moan softly as he bit down on his lip.

"Do you want me to take your boxers down and touch your cock?" Bradley whispered to him. Knowing it was exactly what Jamie was waiting for now.

Jamie nodded his head.

"I like it when I get a verbal answer." Bradley told him, squeezing his cock harder.

"Yes, yes I want you to pull down my boxers and touch my cock." Jamie told him, his face turning bright red.

"You don't have to be embarrassed to tell me what you want. You tell me what you want and depending on what it is I can do it for you." Bradley explained to him softly.

Bradley made him get off his lap for a second. Jamie stood in front of him and watched Bradley move his hands to his waist band.

"I bet your cock looks really nice." Bradley told him, looking into Jamie's eyes as he pulled his boxers down and Jamie slowly stepped out of them.

Jamie looked into his eyes as he saw that his cock was now exposed. Bradley was the one who broke the eye contact first. Looking slowly down his chest and loved how his muscles just showed off for him. He slowly looked down to his cock and loved how thick it was for him.

"For a nice strong man like you you're really shy aren't you?" Bradley asked as he brought his hands to Jamie's cock. A hand on each side of his cock he began giving Jamie's cock a massage.

Rubbing it between his hands as he moved up and down Jamie's hard cock.

"Yes, oh god yes, that feels so good." Jamie whispered to him, closing his eyes. He had sex with woman before but they had never done that to his cock. Not the way Bradley was massaging it.

"I like starting out with a massage first making my partner comfortable and relaxed before we really start." Bradley told him without smiling. It was something that he was good at.

"I wonder if there are jobs out there where you get paid to massage a cock. You would be really good at it." Jamie complimented him as he moaned louder when Bradley rubbed his cock a little harder and a little faster.

"I'm really glad that you like, that you want to try this with me. My first time was good, not the best but really good." Bradley laughed a little. He had no clue what he was doing but he caught on quickly.

Bradley stopped massaging his cock after about ten minutes. His hands getting tired was the only reason he stopped.

Jamie looked at him and wondered what was going to be next. Not sure what to really expect from Bradley.

"Straddle me facing me." Bradley instructed him softly. Seeing the wonder in Jamie's eyes. Jamie did so quickly as he wrapped both of his arms around Bradley's neck just so that he wouldn't fall backward and have Bradley laugh at him.

Bradley pulled his cock out of his speed-o that was getting to be too tight for him. Each time his cock got harder the speed-o got tired. Lowering the speed-o with one hand he brought Jamie's cock to his. Rubbing their heads together. Something that he liked doing often. The head of his cock had always been sensitive so whenever he could he loved to feel the smoothness of another man's cock rubbing against his.

"Mmm, I love that. God that feels so fucking good." Bradley whispered to Jamie. Hearing Jamie moan.

He watched as Jamie closed his eyes and began getting into it. Pushing his cock against Bradley's himself without being told what to do.

"There you go. You're getting it." Bradley was surprised that Jamie would do it on his own. He looked like he had to be instructed to do everything.

"Oh yeah, oh yeah, I have never thought about doing this with a guy. It never crossed my mind but it feels so good." Jamie confessed to him.

"I know it does. I know you're really enjoying it baby. You have some wetness coming out of your hole already." Bradley looked down at the tip of Jamie's cock, knowing that it was his pre-cum and he felt his mouth water like he was looking at a beautiful steak.

Bradley smiled as he quickly laid back on the bed and watched Jamie's eyes widen when he fell on top of Bradley, feeling their cocks mash together hard.

Jamie began grinding the length of his cock against Bradley's like Bradley had done to him in the kitchen. Something that he really enjoyed and wanted to do it him.

"I wonder what you are going to like the best out of this. I'm going to remember to ask you when we are done." Bradley grinned at him, hearing him grunt and moan as he felt Jamie grind his cock harder against his.

Bradley began moaning as well. He loved the pressure that Jamie applied to his cock. He wanted Jamie to do what he felt comfortable doing but he was going to have to sop him soon because he didn't ant to cum all over Jamie's cock. He wanted Jamie to cum for him first and then he would cum for Jamie. It was only right since it was Jamie's first time and all.

"Okay, okay. That's enough teasing. You are going to make me cum." Bradley moaned to him, closing his eyes as he felt the grinding stop.

"What do you want me to do now?" Jamie asked him, not sure which way to go now. He only knew what Bradley had taught him.

Bradley spread his legs as far as they would

go. Looking into Jamie's eyes and seeing that Jamie really wanted to please him now. The shy man in the kitchen was different in the bedroom. His eyes were begging Bradley to let him please him the best he could.

"Lift my legs until you see my ass." Bradley told him softly.

Jamie nodded his head and began lifting up his legs. Bradley didn't help him he could see that Jamie was strong enough.

Jamie smiled when he saw Bradley's ass. Seeing how smooth it was he had never really checked out a man's ass to see how good it looked.

"That's good right there. Can you see my ass?" Bradley asked him.

"Yes." Jamie told him, nodding his head slowly.

"Good. Now take the head of your cock and push it between my ass cheeks. Slowly push your cock into my ass." Bradley moaned to him as he told him how to do it. He always liked giving directions when it came to sex. He had done it twice in the past. The other times he had found someone who was just as gay as he was.

Jamie looked down and pushed his cock between Bradley's ass cheeks like he was told to do. Moving his cock up and down until he found the hole. It was almost like finding a pussy hole to shove his cock into. This excited him even more as he gasped and felt the head of his cock push into a man's ass for the first time.

"You are a pro. You didn't even have to use your hand to guide your cock in." Bradley had watched his hands. They stayed on his legs to make sure that he didn't bring his legs down.

"Here, let me help you out." Bradley told him, putting his legs on both of Jamie's shoulders. Jamie could feel his ankles at his ears.

"That should help you out a lot." Bradley nodded his head.
When he felt Jamie's cock go all the way inside of his ass he smiled and moaned to Jamie. He loved feeling Jamie's cock inside of him.

"Now just like a pussy, its basically the same

thing. Slide your cock in and out of my ass. Fuck my ass just like you would a pussy baby." Bradley whispered to him, biting down on his lip hard. Feeling his cock getting harder just telling him what to do.

Jamie found the confidence he was looking for when he looked down into Bradley's face. The way he bit down on his lip he knew that he was already pleasing him by having his cock deep inside his ass. Jamie actually liked the feeling of it. He soon realized that he liked the feel of it better then he loved having his hard cock inside a wet pussy.

Jamie began fucking him slowly. Seeing a smile go across Bradley's face. Keeping the pace at slow for a little while. He was hoping that he could get Bradley to tell him to fuck him harder before he just went and did it on his own.

"Go faster for me baby." Bradley whispered to him, clearing his throat.

"What? I can't here you?" Jamie asked him, Bradley could see the way Jamie was looking at him and he knew just by looking at him that Jamie was teasing him.

"You aren't suppose to be teasing me the first time you fuck my ass." Bradley told him with a grin on his face.

"What do you want me to do?" Jamie asked him as if he hadn't heard him at all.

"Fuck my ass faster!' Bradley told him, he couldn't just have Jamie tease him. He wanted to feel Jamie cum for him.

Jamie nodded his head, hearing Bradley yell at him gave him more confidence then he thought he would ever have in himself.

Jamie began fucking him just as hard as he could. Wanting to cum inside his ass. Wanting to fill his ass with cum. Closing his eyes and starting to gasp slowly thinking about his cock cumming for Bradley.

"Cum for me baby, I know you are just about there. Fuck my ass Jamie. You are doing such a good job. You look so fucking good sweating for me. I know you really love my ass." Bradley told him.

Bradley heard him grunt and moan loudly for him, knowing that he was hearing everything he was saying to him. Knowing that it was helping Jamie come closer to cumming for him.

"Fuck!" Jamie hollered out to him as he fucked him over and over again. Keeping his eyes closed and smiling.

"You like that don't you baby. You want to cum hard in my ass. Just by the way you are moving in and out of me I know you really want it." Bradley whined and whimpered at him.

"Oh fuck yeah. Oh yeah I want to cum in your ass so hard baby!" Jamie cried out to him. Feeling the cum hit the tip of his cock. Knowing he was just seconds to cumming inside of Bradley's ass.

"Cum for me, please make me a happy man and cum for me." Bradley began begging him over and over again.

"I'm cumming for you! Oh fuck, I'm cumming for you! Giving you what you want and need!" Jamie hollered out to him, feeling his cum shoot into a man's ass for the first time.

"Good job baby. Keep cumming for daddy. I want all your cum up inside my ass." Bradley told him grinding his teeth. He loved the warmth Jamie's cum gave him, loved how Jamie jerked as he finished cumming. He would have to make sure to watch that when they fucked again. He loved having a masculine man jerk the way Jamie was right then. Seeing that even the strongest men did have a weak spot.

Jamie didn't want to take his cock out of Bradley's ass when he was done cumming. He didn't want his play time to end. Now ashamed that he had cum so quickly.

"What's the matter baby?" Bradley asked him when he felt Jamie's soft cock slowly slide out of his ass. Knowing that something was wrong with him.

"My first time cumming for a man and it was too quick." Jamie confessed to him. Letting him know that he wanted to play around longer then what he had.

"Trust me, the first time is always the quickest but you aren't done having fun yet. You still have more ahead of you." Bradley winked at him.

Jamie looked down at Bradley's cock and saw that it was time for him to pleasure him in a different way. Jamie smiled and licked his lips.

"What do you want me to do?" Jamie asked him

"You do whatever you want. I think that you are getting the hang of it now. You're a natural. If you hadn't told me that you never had fucked a man before I never would have known." Bradley told him.

"Are you just pumping me up?" Jamie rolled his eyes at him.

"No, that's one thing that I don't do. I tell the truth. If you suck at fucking my ass I tell you. If I don't think you are doing a good job at sucking my cock I will tell you. That's something that you can count on." Bradley told him seriously. He wasn't going to blow sunshine up his ass by lying to him because then the sex would suck all the time.

Jamie nodded his head and felt Bradley take

his legs down from his shoulders. Bradley winced as he began bending his legs because they were stiff for being up there for so long.

"You okay?" Jamie asked him. He didn't want to start something new and have him hurting to the point where they would have to stop.

"Of course I am." Bradley grinned, moving up the bed. Rolling over on his back and putting his hands behind his head. Waiting for Jamie to do whatever he wanted to him.

Jamie started with spreading his legs as wide as he could. Seeing Bradley's hard cock standing at attention he went to it as if there was a magnetic force bringing his mouth closer and closer to his cock.

Bradley thought that Jamie was mesmerized by his cock. The only thing that he was concentrating on as if the rest of his body wasn't even there.

Jamie didn't know where to start at the head of his cock or lick up from where his cock met his balls.

Jamie looked at him with question marks in his eyes. Bradley knew that he was going to come to him again before he finally decided which way to do it.

"Any way you want to Jamie. Its up to you. You are the one who is at my cock." Bradley whispered to him. Letting him know that he had confidence in him.

Jamie nodded his head and started at the bottom of his cock. Sticking out his tongue and pressing it against the side of Bradley's hard cock he slowly began licking his cock. Licking it until he got to the tip of Bradley's cock.

Taking a quick look he saw Bradley nod his head at him and heard him grunt letting him know that he was dong a good job.

Slowly Jamie slid the tip of his tongue over the head of his cock. Having fun with it. Feeling the smoothness of it against his tongue.

"Fuck Jamie. Are you sure this is your first time?" Bradley asked him softly.

"Yes," Jamie told him and placed his mouth

over the tip of it. Not sure he wanted Bradley's cock completely in his mouth he started out slowly and only began sucking at the head of it. Popping it in and out of his mouth slowly.

"That's good, that feels so good. But do you know what would be really great?" Bradley asked him.

Jamie's heart began pounding thinking that he was doing something wrong already. Hearing Bradley's gentle voice calling out to him.

Jamie stopped sucking at the tip of his cock to listen to him.

"I would like it if you would put more of my cock in your mouth. Slide your wet mouth up and down my cock baby." Bradley told him softly. If it hadn't been Jamie's first time then he would have hollered at him. He would have known the way Bradley liked it come the first time.

Jamie didn't answer him. He was hoping that he didn't have to push Bradley's cock in his mouth all the way. He wasn't sure if he could handle all of it.

Jamie moved his mouth up and down on Bradley's cock, only fitting half of it in his mouth. He didn't want to put too much in his mouth afraid that he would choke on it.

"That's it baby. That is sooo good, god I want to fuck your mouth right now." Bradley told him. Jamie froze for just a minute. He stopped moving his mouth and Bradley could see his eyes widen at what he had just said.

"Don't worry, I won't fuck your mouth. We will work into that slowly, just not tonight." Bradley assured him.

Jamie closed his eyes and felt himself beginning to sweat. Wondering what Bradley's cum would taste like in his mouth.

"Keep sucking my cock. I didn't mean to scare you like that." Bradley apologized to him. Jamie glared at him and sucked furiously on his cock.

He wasn't scared just a little uncertain, taking his frustration out on Bradley's cock and pushing more into his mouth to show Bradley he wasn't scared of his cock.

"I love this baby, fuck my cock with your mouth. Oh yeah, fuck my cock!" Bradley hollered out to him feeling his cum slowly start to travel up to the tip.

"I'm going to cum. I'm going to cum in your mouth, get ready." Bradley warned him. He didn't want to warn Jamie but where it was his first time he knew that he would be pissed if someone came in his mouth for the first time and didn't tell him.

Jamie didn't stop sucking his cock. Curious on how it would feel in his mouth. Wanting to know what it tasted like.

Jamie got his wish. A few seconds later he felt a small flood of cum in his mouth. Moaning with surprise as he found out that he liked the thick liquid in his mouth. He swallowed it down as quickly as he could and felt like he was gagging himself.

"Not so fast. Your first time you shouldn't try to drink it down like water." Bradley laughed at him as he whined out for him.

Jamie slowed down on swallowing the cum.

He did it nice and slow and it worked out better for him that way.

Bradley stopped cumming but he could feel Jamie keep sucking at his cock like he could get more out of him. He loved having a man who didn't know what they were doing for the first time. Thirsty for more. He never had a partner that didn't like his cum.

"Fuck, oh you're tickling me now." Bradley laughed at him. As he felt the cool air hit his cock when Jamie took his mouth away from it slowly.

"How was that?" Jamie asked him softly.

"You did really good. I liked how you sucked my cock but maybe next time you can try to fit all of my cock in your mouth. I think you would look really sexy with all of my cock in your mouth." Bradley told him, he had been a little disappointed that Jamie didn't try to push his mouth down more on his cock. He brushed it off though, knowing that Jamie didn't know what to do with a cock in his mouth. It had been his first time and for the first time as long as Jamie could make him cum then he was doing better then okay.

"I'm a little scared of doing that. I don't want to choke myself." Jamie confessed to him as he sat on the edge of the bed and began putting his boxers back on.

"You can stay in my bed tonight if you want to. I don't have a problem with it. We can watch television and hang out." Bradley told him quickly, he didn't ant Jamie to go home. He wanted to at least cuddle before hand if that was what Jamie wanted to do.

"I don't want Jimmy finding out that I'm here is all. If he sees me here in your room I am sure he's going to put two and two together." Jamie reminded him that his brother was his boss.

Bradley got off the bed and went to the door. He locked the door and smiled at him. Shrugging his shoulders.

"Problem solved. How is he going to know that you are in here huh?" Bradley asked him softly.

"I guess he wont' know that I'm here unless

you tell him." Jamie laughed it off and pulled the sheets back to get into Bradley's bed.

"If you want to go home that's up to you. I'm not going to make you stay here." Bradley wanted him to know that he did have a choice.

"I'm fine with staying. Its a long walk home anyways. I could get up early depending on when Jimmy leaves for the day to meet his clients and get my job done before lunch." Jamie thought about it, setting a goal for himself.

"See it all works out." Bradley laughed at him.

"I have a question for you." Jamie told him thoughtfully as Bradley turned the television on across the room from them.

"What's that?' Bradley asked him.

"Why didn't you stick your cock in my ass? Did you not want to fuck my ass?" Jamie asked him, he blushed and couldn't believe that he was actually asking Bradley that question.

"Oh no, its nothing like that. I don't want to put too much on you. I thought it would be easier for you to suck my cock tonight then to take my cock in your virgin ass." Bradley moaned to him, glad that Jamie had asked him.

"Oh." Jamie told him.

Bradley searched his face and saw that Jamie was really disappointed that Bradley didn't shove it in his ass. He was sure that Jamie was curious but he never thought that Jamie would be looking forward to it. He thought that maybe that first thing in the morning he would fuck Jamie's ass easy. He had lube in his night stand and he knew it would be easier to slick up his cock so that it would push easier into Jamie.

"We will try it in the morning if you want to." Bradley commented flipping through the channels and settling on the news for the night.

"I would love to try it. I want to see if I like it." Jamie nodded his head.

"You liked fucking my ass tonight didn't you?" Bradley asked him. Wanting to make sure that he really enjoyed his first time fucking his ass.

"Oh I really did. It felt so good against my cock. I loved having my cock go in and out of at a fast pace." Jamie grinned at him, nodding his head up and down.

"Good, that's really good." Bradley grunted and smiled at him.

"Would you let me fuck your ass again? Did I do a really good job at it?" Jamie asked, beginning to worry about what Bradley was thinking in the back of his mind.

"Yes, yes. Don't worry about that baby. I think you did really great. I loved having your hard cock inside my ass." Bradley assured him and put his arm around Jamie's waist. Putting his head down on Jamie's hard chest. He loved hearing the loud thumping of Jamie's heart against his ear. It was almost like being able to hear the ocean in a seashell. Hearing the waves crashing against the surf. It was a beautiful noise.

Jamie stiffened up a little. He never cuddled with a man before. It kind of felt funny to him and he knew that he would have to get use to it if they were going to play with each other and Bradley was going to teach him new things.

"What's the matter?" Bradley asked him, feeling him tense up.

"Nothing." Jamie told him quickly.

"Don't lie to me. I know something's the matter with you." Bradley took his head off Jamie's chest and looked into his eyes.

"I'm not use to having a man cuddle with me. It feels kind of weird to me is all." Jamie shrugged him off a little. Hoping that he would get the hint and hoping that Bradley wasn't going to be mad at him.

Bradley didn't say anything. He just shook his head and rolled over. Leaving the television on. Jamie sighed heavily knowing that he had made Bradley mad. He didn't mean to he was just telling the truth.

"Do you want me to leave?" Jamie asked him, he didn't want to leave so late at night but if Bradley wanted him to then he would.

"No." Bradley told him softly, closing his eyes and slowly drifting off to sleep.

Jamie watched Television until he fell asleep

himself. Rolling over and facing Bradley's back. He moved closer to him, not putting his arm around him but if Bradley was still awake he would see that he was at least trying to move in closer to him. It was going to take baby steps when it came to having a man hold him. He was use to a man holding a woman, not a man holding a man.

Early the next morning there was a knock on the door. Jamie heard the knock but didn't say anything. Biting down on his lip as his heart began to race.

"Bradley wake up!" Jimmy hollered, rattling the doorknob and seeing that it was locked. He knew that Bradley liked his privacy but he was surprised that Bradley couldn't hear him banging on the door.

Jamie nudged Bradley softly at first and then began pushing on his shoulder hard. He heard Jimmy banging harder against the door almost knocking it in.

"What!" Bradley finally hollered out.

"I'm going to work. I need you to make sure that the door is going to be unlocked for when Jamie comes over this morning. I don't want him banging down the front door because you can't hear him." Jimmy muttered on the other side of the door.

"Alright, I will see you later." Bradley told him, waking up slowly.

"I mean it Bradley. If he has to bang on that front door and he tells me he had a hard time getting into the house because you wouldn't wake up then you're going to be in trouble." Jimmy told him loudly. The last thing he needed was Bradley to be messing up with the pool boy. He liked Jamie. The only real help that he liked. That was why he was one of his longest employees that he ever had.

"I know!" Bradley hollered to him. Jimmy sighed with frustration as he walked away from the door and went out to his car. Locking the house door. He didn't trust anyone, never knowing if a thug would come into the neighborhood and try to see what houses they could rob. He always had that fear that when he got home that someone would have broken in while he was at work. Knowing that Bradley was up visiting he should have been up when he got ready to go out the door for work.

"Morning." Bradley smiled, sitting up in bed. Glad to see Jamie's face first thing in the morning. He had slept good through the night.

"Morning. I think that I should get dressed and start cleaning the pool. Looks like I'm going to have to put my jeans on that are down by the pool." Jamie told him, he wanted to start as soon as he could so that he could get the job done and be able to relax for a little while.

"I thought maybe you would like to have a cup of coffee first before you started working. What time do you usually get here?" Bradley asked him getting out of bed and putting on a pair of boxers that he found on his side of the bed from yesterday morning.

"I usually don't come around until ten." Jamie guessed and shrugged his shoulders. It was a close enough estimation on time.

"Here it is five in the morning and you are worried about getting to work. Relax for a few hours. Five hours before you usually get to work." Bradley rolled his eyes and walked to the bedroom door unlocking it.

Jamie put on the pair of boxers that Bradley had given to him. A smile on his face as he went to go use the bathroom. When Jamie came out Bradley went into the bathroom himself and came back out to make a pot of coffee.

Jamie opened the door to the deck and started down the stairs. Bradley sighed and shook his head, turning the coffee pot on he went down the stairs to see if he could convince him to just have a cup of coffee with him.

When he got down to the bottom of the steps he saw Jamie bent over getting the net under the deck. He smiled as he felt his cock getting hard inside his boxers.

Tip-toeing as he got closer behind him he pressed his cock against Jamie's ass and moaned softly as he continued pressing his cock through his boxers against Jamie.

"You took be by surprise." Jamie looked over his shoulder and grinned at him.

"Can I at least have you take the time to let me stick my growing cock inside your tight ass?" Bradley whispered to him.

Jamie nodded his head at him. Feeling Bradley pull his boxers down. He loved how Jamie's ass looked nice and smooth.

He brought his hands to his ass cheeks and rubbed them, grunting and closing his eyes as he felt the smoothness of his ass.

"Do you like that?" Jamie asked him in a low voice.

"I don't like your ass, I love your ass Jamie. Feels really good." Bradley grunted and slapped his ass cheek lightly, hearing Jamie cry out for him.

"You want me to spank you harder baby?' Bradley teased him.

"Yessss." Jamie hissed at him. Raising his ass up a little, wanting to feel Bradley's hand slap against his ass again.

"Good boy. You know what you like huh?" Bradley chuckled and bit down on his lip.

It wasn't the way Bradley had wanted to fuck his ass. Thinking about the lube that was in his night stand. He didn't want to break the mood now and rush into the house to get it. Spanking Jamie harder as he brought his other hand to his mouth and began getting it wet with his tongue. Rubbing his cock up and down and getting it wet. He spit in the palm of his hand and rubbed the spit on the head of his cock.

"Are you ready for my cock Jamie?" Bradley asked him, thinking he had enough wetness on the head of his cock so that it wouldn't hurt him when he pushed inside of him.

"I'm ready. I want to know what it feels like." Jamie told him, getting excited as he felt the head of Bradley's cock push between his ass cheeks.

Jamie almost begged for Bradley's cock seeing that he was taking too long to put his cock inside of his ass.

"Only reason why I am going so easy is its your first time and I don't want to hurt you when I stretch your asshole with my cock." Bradley explained to him. Rubbing and caressing Jamie's ass cheeks.

Jamie closed his eyes as he felt Bradley enter him a little. It did hurt but Jamie closed his eyes tight and gritted his teeth together. Hoping that it wouldn't hurt as much when Bradley put his cock all the way in his ass.

"Are you alright?" Bradley asked him, seeing that Jamie was awfully quiet.

"It hurts a little." Jamie told him truthfully.

"The first time usually does. If you want me to stop I will. Just give me the word and I will stop." Bradley whispered to him feeling bad for hurting him at all.

Bradley remembered how much it hurt his ass when he had a cock inside of it. Jamie didn't know it but he was lucky to have someone like Bradley fucking his ass. The first time he started out the man he was with wasn't easy at all. He was horny as fuck and just slammed his cock deep inside his ass. He felt dizzy and started seeing stars when the man fucked him. He even cried a little because of the pain he had felt.

Bradley pushed his cock into Jamie little by little, taking his time and controlling his breathing. He didn't hear Jamie cry out in pain. Which made him feel better about hurting him.

"Are you still okay?" Bradley asked him when his cock was completely inside of him.

"Yes, oh yes. I'm okay." Jamie told him hurriedly.

"The best way to deal with it the first time is make sure you regulate your breathing. Don't hold your breath the way you are doing. Breathe slowly." Bradley told him softly, kissing each ass cheek and rubbing his nose around on his ass cheeks.

He heard Jamie breathing regularly as he watched his cock and only pulled it out enough to where he could almost see the head of his cock. Not wanting to hurt him again. He had learned that if the cock came all the way out and then reentered it hurt more and more.

Bradley moaned as he pushed his cock into him again. A little quicker, thinking that he would hear Jamie yelp.

"Am I hurting you?" Bradley asked him since he didn't hear anything coming out of Jamie's mouth.

"No, its starting to feel better." Jamie smiled, telling him the truth. He began to enjoy it more and more as Bradley began fucking him more and more.

Bradley put his hands on Jamie's hips and began fucking him a little faster each time. Hoping that he was going to hear some kind of noise out of Jamie.

"Your cock feels good in my ass." Jamie gasped a few minutes later. Feeling his cock getting hard as he whimpered to Bradley for more.

"Your ass is so nice and tight for my cock. I love how tight your ass is for me." Bradley grunted and moaned.

"Baby, please fuck my ass hard. I know you

want to. Fuck my ass hard with that thick cock of yours." Jamie begged him, needing to feel it more. Wanting to feel it more, he was beginning to shake just thinking about what it would be like with cum deep in his ass.

Bradley fucked him faster and faster. Not as fast as he could because he had to remember it was Jamie's first time. He had to keep reminding himself silently that he had to calm down and keep pace so that Jamie would cry like he had.

"Fuck Jamie, god Jamie!" Bradley hollered out to him.

"Yeah? You about to cum? I can't wait to feel your cum deep in my ass baby. Cum in my ass, don't hold any of it back." Jamie begged him, he wanted the complete load up inside his ass.

"I'm........I'm going to cum in your ass Jamie........I won't hold any back.......Fuck I need you and I want you." Bradley began gasping and moaning. Pushing his cock in one more time and pushing it as far as he could he squirted his cum deep inside Jamie's ass.

"Fuck! Oh my god!" Jamie screamed out as loud as he could.

"Am I hurting you baby?' Bradley almost jumped, his cock almost coming out of Jamie's ass before he could get done cumming.

"No, I love it. It surprised me is all. That warm liquid filling my ass. My first time and I didn't think it would ever feel this good deep inside of me. I fucking love your cum in me." Jamie explained quickly, not wanting Bradley take his cock out of him.

"I'm so glad that you love it sweetie. I love how your ass feels. Fuck me!" Bradley hollered out as he felt his cock squirt the last of its cum inside his ass.

"That was so good. So fucking good." Jamie told him, catching his breath. Wishing that Bradley would cum more for him.

He sighed when Bradley took his cock out of his ass. As he tried to stand up straight his ass felt sore and he knew he would be walking funny most of the day.

"You'll be alright." Bradley laughed at him as he groaned when he stood straight up and saw that he had a funny look on his face.

"Someone's awake for me. I was hoping that you would be by the time I got done cumming in your ass. Come to papa." Bradley looked down at his cock and noticed it was harder then the night before.

Jamie watched him as Bradley hit his knees and brought his mouth to his cock. He moaned loudly as he felt Bradley's mouth move quickly back and forth across his cock. Bradley was fucking his cock hard with his mouth. Wanting to taste his cum as soon as he could.

"God! Oh fuck!" Jamie hollered out to him. Watching his cock move in and out of Bradley's mouth.

Bradley licked and nibbled the head of his cock each time he popped it out of his mouth. He sounded like a wildcat that hadn't been fed in a week. Grunting louder each time he felt Jamie's cock hit the back of his throat.

"No wonder why you wanted to fuck my mouth last night. God damn! You just take right over when you really want something." Jamie whined at him.

Bradley moaned when he heard Jamie gasping and wanting to cum for him. He knew the sounds of almost cumming but what surprised him was when his cock started jerking in his mouth and he loved how it pulsed inside his mouth.

A few minutes more and Bradley got exactly what he wanted. He felt Jamie cum for him. He sucked harder and faster as Jamie's cock.

"Mmm, fuck baby. That is what I want right there. That is all I want!" Jamie cried out to him. Loving the way his cock felt inside Bradley's mouth.

Jamie felt his cock explode inside Bradley's mouth. He felt how Bradley swallowed his cum down quickly, wondering why he didn't gag on it. Remembering that Bradley had told him that it would take practice wondering just how much Practice Bradley had sucking a man's cock and swallowing his cum.

When he was done Bradley got up from his knees with a smile on his face. He wrapped his arms around Jamie and held him tightly. He felt Jamie's arms go around him and it felt so good for them to hold each other.

"That was wonderful. Your cum tastes soo good baby. I didn't want to stop sucking that beautiful cock of yours." Bradley whispered into his ear.

"I loved the way your cock felt inside my ass Bradley. Thank you for going easy with me. I loved every minute of it. Even the small pain, along with pleasure there has to be a little bit of pain when you have something new done to you." Jamie explained to him and kissed him on the side of the neck. Nibbling on Bradley's neck just a little. Hearing Bradley moan against his ear glad that he could tease him a little bit.

"Come on pool boy, can I convince you to have a cup of coffee with me now?" Bradley pulled away from him a little so that he could look into Jamie's eyes.

"I think that would be just fine." Jamie replied, nodding his head.

Jamie and Bradley put their boxers back on and quickly came out from under the deck. Glad that it was just the two of them. Bradley had to find a way to be able to stay at Jimmy's house. He couldn't just walk away from Jamie after a week or two. He wanted to have more fun with him, knowing that he would miss him too much if he went back home.

"What are you thinking about?" Jamie asked him when they entered the kitchen and sat down at the table. Knowing that Bradley was thinking about something because he was quiet until that moment.

"I was thinking about staying another week here. I mean we are having fun getting to know each other. I could come on on the weekends and spend some time with you." Bradley told him thinking about it more as he took two coffee cups out of the cupboard and looked at Jamie.

"Just black." Jamie told him.

"So what do you think?" Bradley asked him, filling his cup and bringing it over to him. Handing the hot cup to Jamie slowly so that he didn't spill any hot liquid on him.

"I think that would be great. We could get to know each other more." Jamie agreed with him as he blew on his hot coffee.

"Good. We will start out like that for now." Bradley didn't want to push him into anything he didn't want. Thinking about it Bradley wasn't sure that he could leave his own home and friends. Living with Jimmy had been hell at times when he had to move in because he couldn't take care of himself.

When Jamie got done with his coffee he put it in the sink. Knowing that he had to get to work like he did every morning.

Bradley kissed him on the cheek before he headed out the door. He watched as Jamie went down the stairs and put his jean shorts on. If Jimmy had come home right then and there he wouldn't have known that something happened between them. He couldn't let Jimmy find out what they were doing he didn't want to risk Jimmy firing Jamie. He didn't think that his brother would like him messing around with the pool boy. He had already been warned when he was first told about Jamie. Jimmy didn't want him to be alarmed when a kid came by the house.

Bradley went out onto the deck. The sun was already threatening a hot day. Hotter then the day before as he watched Jamie get into the pool with the net that cleaned the pool. He felt bad for Jamie in a way. Jimmy was very picky about how his things were to be kept clean. When Jimmy told him that the pool boy cleaned the pool every day he thought that Jimmy was only joking around with him but when he saw Jimmy not smiling at him he knew that he was being serious. Shaking his head and telling Jimmy that was too much for such a long pool.

"Make sure you get everything out of that pool. Not even a speck of dirt in there!" Bradley called from the railing of the deck.

Jamie laughed at him and gave him the finger

as he continued with work. Happy that Bradley would find the time to watch him work.

"You better make sure boss man don't see you doing that. You'll get into trouble." Bradley teased him and laughed loudly.

Bradley went back into the house and put on some swimming trunks and went back out, this time going down to the pool. He sat on the edge just dangling his feet in the water. He loved the cold water against his warm feet.

"Stay out of my way." Jamie told him, when he heard Bradley splashing his feet in the water. Making ripples in the once calm pool.

Bradley was sitting there just watching Jamie. He was hoping that by the time he left Jimmy's house that he could tell Jimmy what was going on. He didn't want to hide anything from his brother, keeping things a secret never worked out for anyone.

He was going to talk to Jimmy that night. Not telling him about what had happened but asking questions to see how he would feel about him going after Jamie. If it was a bad outcome then he wouldn't tell him, seeing that Jamie liked his job. Even though Jimmy liked to be strict about the pool he didn't hear Jamie complain once since he had been at the house about keeping Jimmy happy.

"Tonight's a test night. If he's not too upset about me liking Jamie then I will continue with the conversation. If he doesn't like that then he would drop it. He would rather keep what was going on between them a secret then to have Jamie lose his job.

"What are you thinking about over there?" Jamie asked him, looking over his shoulder and seeing that he was deep in thought.

"Nothing, just thinking about how hot its going to be today. Nothing for you to worry about." Bradley grinned at him. Looking over in his direction.

"You are kind of a distraction you know. I know you're watching me while I work. That's fine but if you are going to watch me you might as well find something to talk about to make the time go by faster. You know like yesterday." Jamie pointed out to him.

Bradley slipped into the pool and swam over to Jamie. Treading water in the deep end he kissed the back of Jamie's neck. Licking up and down it.

"That is more a distraction." Jamie grunted to him. Closing his eyes for a brief second enjoying the wetness of Bradley's tongue.

"Well we could talk about sex and what we are going to do to each other the next time." Bradley moaned and bit down on his neck before swimming away from him.

Jamie shook his head and smiled. Never had he thought he would enjoy being pleased by a man. Now that Bradley had showed him just how good it could be he couldn't think about the girl who ditched him, he didn't care what the girls excuse was when she called him or saw him he would pretend that he didn't even know her. Feeling his cock move inside his shorts, a grin from ear to ear as he thought about shoving his cock into Bradley's ass. Thinking that the next time he got to Bradley's ass he would lick him and shove his tongue so far into his ass that Bradley would beg for his cock. He felt his cock getting harder as he thought about Bradley begging for him. He could hear Bradley's voice as he begged for his hard cock.

The End.

OTHER HOT EROTIC ROMANCE BOOKS YOU MIGHT BE INTERESTED IN:

LESBIAN:

Look inside ↓

Erotica Lesbian First Time: Alison's First Time

When Jennifer sleeps over and they get ready to call it a night Alison sees that Jennifer put a porn movie on. Getting under the covers she watched it, out of the corner of her eye she saw that Jennifer couldn't take her eyes away from the screen. Seeing a woman sucking a man's cock and then another woman entering the picture Jennifer begins asking Alison questions. Will it lead to more then just watching a porn movie? Cum and see if more will happen.

Look inside ↓

Lesbian Erotica: Jackie's Lesbian Erotic Romance Sex Story

Jackie has had the worst of luck; she was sent by her family to go to church on Christmas Eve. As an atheist and a lesbian, she's had the worst scenario come up. But when an old flame and former best friend from high school pops up, it turns out things get even better between the two. They go out, and things soon become steamy. But will Jackie be able to fall in love with her, and will her former crush Caitlin accept her love? And what will her parents think when they hear about this? Will they approve of the relationship, or will religious ties turn her away?

Lesbian Erotica: Hot & Erotic Lesbian Neighbors

Shelly has a secret wish that one day she will find a woman that would want to explore with her. Deep down Shelly wants to know what it feels like to have her pussy licked and her tits sucked on. Never knowing if that would come because all of her friends were straight. She wants to feel a woman's tongue down at her pussy and cum in a woman's mouth. When Shelly gives the next door neighbor Andrea a ride to the store because her snow is stuck in the snow Shelly doesn't think anything of it. Just helping someone out. Then Andrea comes over and starts to hang out with her, what Andrea reveals about herself shocks Shelly and knows that she's going to have her wish come true after all.

GAY:

Gay Romance MM: A Gay College Lesson

Ben knows that he's failing English class. His professor was always warning him that he had to bring his grades up. Ben knows that college is so much different then high school where he actually has to pay attention and turn his work in. When his professor makes him stay after class Ben thinks that he's just going to get another lecture, but what Ben gets is so much more and more to his liking.

Gay Erotica MMM: The Salon

When Erin starts working at a hair salon he finds out that Julian, the guy he works with his gay. At the end of the day things get hot at the kitchen table while they wait for their food inside Erin's house. As they continue Erin finds that he is falling hard for Julian but what happens when Julian doesn't show up for work a few days later? Will Erin turn to someone else? You'll have to read to find out for yourself!

Gay Erotic Romance Stories: Tom Discovers He's Gay

Tom never once thought about a man in a sexual way before. Not until Tasha had introduces him to her uncle Martin. When Tom's car won't start and Tom gets a ride home from Martin things start to heat up. Tom realizes that he can't get enough for Martin's cock no matter what price he has to pay he's willing to get caught when he invites Martin to stay the night in his room......

Gay Erotica: Finding Love In Another Man's Arms

While Clay is out running errands on Eric's day off Eric gets bored and decides to fold Clay's clean clothes that are in the basket outside his door. When Eric brings the basket into Clay's bedroom he decides that to be nice he would make his friends bed. When he pulls the sheet back and sees a magazine that at first glance he thinks its a dirty magazine about women, taking a closer look he sees that its a gay magazine. Putting the magazine back in the exact spot he found it and covering it the way Clay had it Eric can't help but wonder if deep down Clay is gay. The next day Eric calls out of work sick and Clay offers to give him a massage before the day is through. As Eric gets turned on by Clay's hands on his body he makes his move. Finding out why Clay has the dirty magazine in his bedroom to begin with........

Erotic Romance MM: First Time Gay - Hottie In The Pool

Jamie had been working for Jimmy for three summers in a row so far. Working as a pool boy and getting a lot of money for cleaning the pool every day. Jimmy wanted to make sure that his pool stayed nice and clean in case he had people coming over unexpectedly or when he had a group of people come over for parties. When Jimmy's gay brother Bradley comes for a visit he introduces the two of them to each other. Bradley begins to like him right away starting a conversation with him when Jimmy leaves unexpectedly to see a client. While Jimmy's away Bradley thinks its okay for the mice to play.

Gay Erotic Romance: Two Men In A Coffee Shop

When Tony meets Alexander after a break up with his boyfriend he talks to Alexander about what had happened briefly in his last relationship. Little does Tony know the more they talk with one another the more he finds they have in common with each other. Like one common factor that they both are gay. Tony has never told his parents that he is gay, afraid that he will cause them a heart attack. Sliding that to the back of his mind Tony thinks that it's time to move on with his life and hopes that Alexander is there to move on with him.

TABOO:

Erotic Romance Sex Stories Collection: A Babysitter's Erotica Fantasy

Silver-tongued Lexi Mandalay is celebrating her 18th birthday with no job, no future, and her only hope of making it after graduation is to use her wits and her looks to make it big in her dream career in fashion design.

Her parents leaving to travel abroad isn't helping matters either, and Lexi has to stay with her crazy Aunt Freddie until she starts Junior College, or its off the another country for good.

Lexi hears the babysitting biz is booming and her best friend Gillian sets her up with a gig to sit for the daughter of aging TV actress Lucy Deschannel. Everything is copacetic until Lexi is caught snooping by Lucy's hunky ad exec brother John Oliver. John and Lexi share an instant chemistry as John tempts Lexi to explore her secret fantasies about pleasure—and pain.

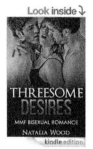

MMF BISEXUAL ROMANCE: Threesome Desires

Married couple Trey and Sophia are co-workers in love, but sometimes find themselves bored and distractions. They both have fantasies, but never really expect to play them out - that is until Ray enters the picture. An office meeting brings the three of them behind closed doors and sparks begin to fly. Lustful urges surface between them and forbidden longings are revealed not only between Sophia and the guys, but also between Trey and Ray. Will Sophia and Trey risk jeopardizing their marriage for indulgence into a world of taboo menage desires?

Taboo Sex Stories For Adults: An Erotica Romance Collection (Book 1 of 3)

Kellie has a fascination with her boss Brian. Trying to find the courage to come up with a way to seduce him. Shy Kellie isn't so shy when she finds out that his secret is that he's gay. As soon as she finds out she goes to blackmailing him. Her demands get stronger when she finds out as long as she has the evidence with her that Brian will do anything she asks of him.

Taboo Sex Stories For Adults: An Erotica Romance Collection (Book 2 of 3)

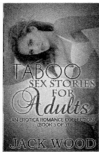

Taboo Sex Stories For Adults: An Erotica Romance Collection (Book 3 of 3)
Brian waits for Kyle to come over so he can put his idea into action. Hoping that he finds some dirt on Kellie he's going out of the blue to her house with Kyle without her knowing. They end up getting the surprise of a life time when they show up. After they get the evidence they need it feels like they are on a non-stop roller coaster where they control all twist and turns.

Erotic Romance Sex Stories Collection: A Womans Erotica Fantasy

Leigha Peyton is a talented Private Investigtor with a strong vendetta against dishonest men. Naturally, when master thief Pierce Logan crosses her path, charming her into oblivion, she goes after him with a vengeance. When a failed police chase leaves her hostage to the very man she hoped to bring down, will she hold tight to her grudge? Or will the mystery man with a murky past steal her heart?

Babysitter Erotica: Obsessed With His Mouth (Part 1 of 3)

Landing a job babysitting the Trevor twins is the best thing to happen to Alice in a long time. The girls are lovable - if a little wild, the pay is through the roof, and their father...well, Liam Trevor is about the most luscious thing she's ever laid eyes on. The authority he commands both in the courtroom and his own household intimidates her as much as it tantalizes her, and after finding a secret file in his study, she discovers why. Liam's particular brand of intimacy involves her complete subjugation - and the punishment for her curiosity is capitally wicked.

TABOO: Alisha's Erotic Romance Trip

Alisha is a normal woman who gets a chance to finally take a vacation after a hard season at the office. She goes there, but after a mishap with the registration area, she's unsure if she can stay. However, one man swoops down and comes to the rescue, a devilishly handsome man named Martin Powers. Alisha immediately falls for this man, but little does she know that he's hiding a secret. Can Alisha uncover the secret of this man? And what will that mean for their relationship? Will it last, or will it turn into nothing more than just a fling in an exotic location...

Bisexual Erotica: A MFF Bisexual Threesome Starring Sarah, Todd, and Julie

When Julie comes up with a great idea for a threesome Sarah decides to go along with it. Julie asks Todd to come over and help her paint her bedroom as an excuse to get him to go over to her house. They begin flirting at work and Todd thinks he's going to have the chance to have sex with her when they get to her house. To Todd's surprise her roommate is just as pretty as Julie. Not knowing what's in store for him he is just happy that he agreed to help Julie with the her painting project. Later on he finds out that he's the luckiest man alive.

CONTEMPORARY:

Captivated By A Girl: The Dark Secret Marked Forever

Shane is on the verge of questioning everything about his job and his life when he decides on a whim to pick up a young hitchhiker named Lily in the rain. But as their relationship develops and they spend a weekend in a secluded cabin on the Olympic Peninsula, she teaches him how to connect with another human being. However, Lily is harboring a dark secret of her own, which may prevent them from being together.

Dirty Secret Behind A Kiss: A Young Adult Romance Series

Aubrey is living up the single life and dating who she wants, when she wants but deep down she dreams of belonging to one perfect guy. It could be Benton, but then his best friend Jalen, the bad boy and every nice girl's wet dream, makes a pass at Aubrey. When Benton finds out it sends chaos through his budding relationship with Aubrey. As she searches for the right guy Aubrey realizes too late that it's Benton and she'll do almost anything to get him back."

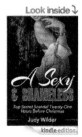

Look inside ↓

A Sexy & Shameless Top Secret Scandal Twenty-One Hours Before Christmas

Felicia had always made a living out of shoplifting. She would scope out shops in small business areas. Never once getting caught. She would sell the things she took to make cash for the things she needed. When Felicia gets the idea to hit up the mall she meets an older man named Jefferey and begins flirting with him. When she finds out that Jefferey has a clothing shop that sells sexy lingerie she gets closer to him. Hoping to gain his trust. But when she's caught taking clothing from his store she automatically thinks that she's going to go to jail until Jefferey gives her two options. He is so attracted to Felicia he gives her the option to go to jail or to sexually pleasure him. Felicia makes the right choice. The sex between the two of them will make you cum back for more!